MISHMASH

Russian text Корней Чуковский, Наследники
Copyright © 2011
Illustrations by Francesca Yarbusova Copyright © 2011
English translation by Luba Golburt
with Lisa Little © 2011
Rovakada LLC. Copyright © 2011

www.norsteinstudio.com
www.norshteyn.ru

ISBN 978-0-9845867-4-5 $17.95

Publisher: Rovakada Publishing
Manufacturing location: Shenzhen, China
Production date: June 10, 2011
Batch number: Rova 201106101
Materials used in this publication are tested
according to The Consumer Product Safety
Improvement Act (CPSIA)

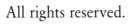

MISHMASH

Korney Chukovsky
Illustrations by Francesca Yarbusova

Translated by Luba Golburt with Lisa Little

Rovakada Publishing
San Francisco
2011

Once the kittens set up a howl:
"How much longer can we meow?!
We'd much rather grunt like piglets:
Oink-oink-oink."

Next the ducklings followed suit:
"Quacking fits us not one bit!
We'd much rather croak like frogs:
Ribbit-ribbit-ribbit."

So the piglets took to meowing:
Meow-meow-meow.

And the kittens started oinking:
Oink-oink-oink.

And the ducklings set to croaking:
Ribbit-ribbit-ribbit.

And the chickens started quacking:
Quack-quack-quack.

Next the sparrow hopped along,
But now he sang the cow's song:
Moo-o-o!

Then the bear hurried in,

And began roaring:
Cock-a-doodle-doo!

Then the cuckoo chimed in, too,
"Do I have to say 'cuckoo'?
I'd much rather bark and woof,
Like a dog or a wolf."

And only the rabbit,
Goody Mr. Two-shoes:
Would not meow,
And would not oink,
But lay by his cabbage,
And in his rabbit language,
Urged all those silly critters
To behave themselves:

"Let the meowing kind
Never moo!
Let the mooing kind
Never meow!
Never will a crow be a cow!
Never will a frog fly in the clouds!"
The rabbit did all that he could.
But the merry little critters,
All those bear cubs and piglets
Were still up to no good.

The fish walked around on the ground.
The toads flew about on a cloud.
The mice caught a cat
And set him in a trap.

The little foxes
Snatched some matches.
To the sea they swiftly raced,
And they set the sea ablaze.

From the flames, out of the sea,
Jumped a whale and cried:
"Help me-e-e-e!
Call the firemen right now!
Put this fire out somehow!"

So the alligator came,
And worked hard to quell the flames
With pancakes and pies,
And mushrooms and fries.

The chickens brought a barrel,
The fish fetched a ladle,
The frogs came with a pail.
They kept dousing the fire,
But the flames only burned higher.
They kept pouring the water,
But the sea only grew hotter.

Then a butterfly
Flew so gently by.
And the fire started dying –
And… died out.

Then the animals rejoiced!
Laughing and singing
Clapping and dancing,
Stomping and prancing.

The geese started honking:
Honk-honk-honk!
The kittens started meowing:
Meow-meow-meow!
The birds started chirping:
Chirrup-chirrup-chirrup!
The horses started neighing:
Neigh-neigh-neigh!
The flies started buzzing:
Buzzzz-buzzzz-buzzzz!
The frogs started croaking:
Ribbit-ribbit-ribbit!
The ducklings started quacking:
Quack-quack-quack!
The piglets started oinking:
Oink-oink-oink!

Singing their lullabies
To our little one:
"Rockabye, baby, rockabye!"

Korney Chukovsky (1882 - 1969) was a renowned Russian writer, poet, translator, influential literary critic and essayist. He wrote his first children's poem, *The Crocodile* (1916) at the age of 34. Since that time he was primarily known for his children's stories, both in poetry and prose. Subsequently, they were adapted for theater, animated and live-action films, opera and ballet. With more than 300 million copies printed and translated into 87 languages, Korney Chukovsky is one of the most published Russian authors. Chukovsky was a prolific translator, having translated English writers such as Walt Whitman, Rudyard Kipling and Mark Twain into Russian, among others.

Francesca Yarbusova (1942) is a distinguished Russian artist, animated film art director, illustrator. Along with her husband, famous animator and director Yuri Norstein, she was the co-creator of memorable and award-winning films. The film *Tale of Tales* was named the Best Animated Film of All Time by the American Academy of Motion Picture Arts and Sciences in Los Angeles in 1984 and at the Zagreb International Animation Festival in 2002. In 2003, an international film jury in Tokyo declared their other film, *Hedgehog in the Fog*, to be the Best Animated Film of All Time. Exhibitions of Francesca Yarbusova's artwork successfully showed in museums of Russia, France, and Japan, among others. She is the recipient of the Great Gold Medal of the Russian Academy of Fine Art.